Going to Grandma's

For Barry—my very own Travelin' Bear! —P. H.

SIMON SPOTLIGHT
An imprint of Simon & Schuster Children's Publishing Division
1230 Avenue of the Americas
New York, New York 10020
This Simon Spotlight edition October 2015
Text and illustrations copyright © 2001 by Simon & Schuster, Inc.
The names and depictions of Raggedy Ann and Raggedy Andy are trademarks of Simon & Schuster, Inc.
SIMON SPOTLIGHT, READY-TO-READ, and colophon are registered trademarks of Simon & Schuster, Inc.
For information about special discounts for bulk purchases, please contact Simon & Schuster Special Sales
at 1-866-506-1949 or business@simonandschuster.com
Manufactured in the United States of America 0915 LAK
2 4 6 8 10 9 7 5 3 1
Library of Congress Cataloging-in-Publication Data
Hall, Patricia, 1948-
Going to Grandma's / by Patricia Hall ; illustrated by Kathryn Mitter.— 1st ed.
p. cm. — (Classic Raggedy Ann & Andy) (Ready-to-read)
Summary: When Raggedy Ann and Andy accompany Marcella on an airplane trip to visit her grandmother, they
are placed in the baggage compartment, where they play with a teddy bear they meet.
[1. Dolls—Fiction. 2. Air travel—Fiction. 3. Airplanes—Fiction. 4. Teddy bears—Fiction. 5. Toys—Fiction.]
I. Mitter, Kathy, ill. II. Title. III. Series. IV. Series: Ready-to-read
PZ7.H147515 Go 2001
[E]—dc21
2001029451
ISBN 978-1-4814-5077-5 (hc)
ISBN 978-1-4814-5076-8 (pbk)
ISBN 978-1-4814-5078-2 (eBook)
RaggedyAnnBooks.com

RAGGEDY ANN & ANDY
Going to Grandma's

PEACHTREE

by Patricia Hall
illustrated by Kathryn Mitter

Ready-to-Read

Simon Spotlight
New York   London   Toronto   Sydney   New Delhi

"We are going to Grandma's!"
Marcella said to
Raggedy Ann and Andy.

"It is our first plane ride.
You can ride inside my suitcase
for now.
When we get on the plane
you can come out to play,"
said Marcella.

Marcella's suitcase did not
fit in its space on the plane.
"Your suitcase is too big!"
said the flight attendant.
"But do not worry!
We will put it
with the other suitcases
under the plane."

It was time for take-off.
Marcella buckled her seat belt.

"I am going to Grandma's!" she said.
She was very excited.

"Everything is so small!"
said Marcella.
"Is that my house?"

Marcella was having a lot of fun.
She did not miss her dolls.

"Time to play!" said Raggedy Andy.
They stepped out of the suitcase.
"This is not on the plane!"
said Raggedy Ann.
"Where are we?"
asked the Raggedys.

"You are in the bottom of the plane,"
said a voice.
A fuzzy, brown bear peeked out
at the Raggedys.

"Hello! I am Travelin' Bear!
Who are you?"

"We are Raggedy Ann and
Raggedy Andy," said the dolls.
"We live with Marcella,
and we are going to Grandma's!"
said Raggedy Andy.
"Where do you live?"
asked Raggedy Ann.
"I live on this airplane!"
said Travelin' Bear.

"I will show you around!"
said Travelin' Bear.
"Let's go!"
First he showed the Raggedys
how to swing.

Next he showed them
how to slide.

"I love to fly!"
said Travelin' Bear.

"Whee!" giggled the Raggedys.
"We love to fly too!"

"You can stay with me
on the plane," said Travelin' Bear.
"We would have lots of fun!"
"No, thank you,"
said Raggedy Ann.
"We would miss Marcella."
"And," said Raggedy Andy,
"we are going to Grandma's!"

The airplane slowed down.

"Buckle your seat belts!"
said the pilot.
"The airplane is landing!"

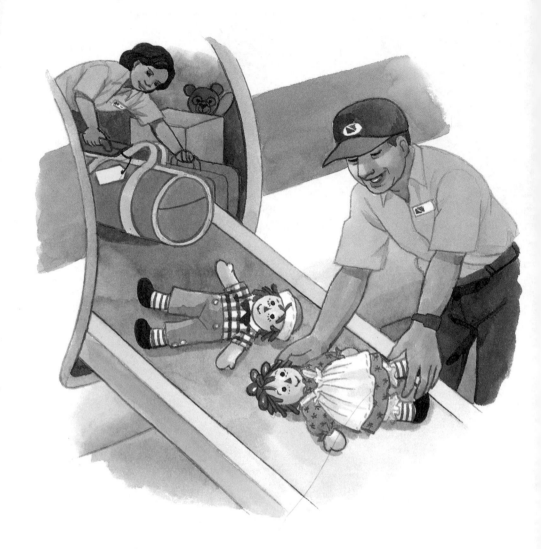

A nice man unloaded the suitcases.
"Look who I found!" he laughed.
He picked up the rag dolls.

Marcella's grandma met her
at the airport.
Marcella was happy to see her.
She told Grandma all about her trip.

Then Marcella remembered
the Raggedys!

"Are these dolls yours?"
the nice man asked.
"Raggedy Ann! Raggedy Andy!"
cried Marcella.
"I am so glad to see you!"

"I am sorry you fell
out of my suitcase," Marcella said.

"I hope you did not miss me."

Raggedy Ann and Andy
just smiled.
Because everyone knows
that rag dolls do not talk!